THE STO-
RY OF
MY ACCI-
DENT
IS
OURS

THE STO-RY OF MY ACCI-DENT IS OURS

RACHEL LEVITSKY

first edition | first printing

This edition first published in paperback by Futurepoem books
P.O. Box 7687 JAF Station, NY, NY 10116
www.futurepoem.com

Executive Editor: Dan Machlin
Managing Editor: Jennifer Tamayo
Additional Editors: Chris Martin & Ted Dodson

Cover design: Mickel Design (www.mickeldesign.com)
Typesetting: HR Hegnauer (www.hrhegnauer.com)
Typefaces: Custom Font by Mickel Design (Spine & Back Cover); Caslon (Text)

Printed in the United States of America on acid-free paper

This project is supported in part by the New York State Council on the Arts with the support of Governor Andrew Cuomo and the New York State Legislature, as well as by individual donors and subscribers. Additional support was provided by a Face Out grant, funded by The Jerome Foundation and administered by The Council of Literary Magazines and Presses and a Pratt Institute Mellon Foundation Grant. Futurepoem books is the publishing program of Futurepoem, Inc., a New York state-based 501(c)3 non-profit organization dedicated to creating a greater public awareness and appreciation of innovative literature.

Distributed to the trade by Small Press Distribution, Berkeley, California
Toll-free number (U.S. only): 800.869.7553
Bay Area/International: 510.524.1668
orders@spdbooks.org
www.spdbooks.org

From Almost Any Angle

We woke into the world—
All at once and all one way like characters you'd see in a science fiction movie, without parents, cloned for the purpose of replacing the organs of the rich, or jailed indefinitely and repeatedly for our childbearing ability. We had the appearance of arriving whole, the sets of our features predetermined and complete.

Defined by limitation—
We were kept away from history by serial clearances: slums, streets, the poor, then the rich, then the home, then the street, then the neighborhood, then the mall, and then the mall. (The mall.)

We recognized each other—
We communicated by way of a vacant look in our eyes and sophistication in our speech when we had the energy to speak. We were not quite like creatures in zombie movies that were popular again in our time. We didn't join in the common cause of destroying one another, or making another more like us. We lacked killer instinct. We doubted the necessity, that what we were should be reproduced or multiplied. We were ignorant of

what we were, uncertain about the ways we did have, what they were and how they'd come to be.

What we knew better than what we were and the ways we had was all that we were strange to. We were strange to the ways of smiles—smiles possessed by the ones on television, big and radiant, infused with all the light in the room from which their image was cast, smiles worn by the ones outside in front of the church, placidly making their way through those who'd get in their way of smiling and smiles exchanged by the two who were passing each other, in a case where one is walking down a sidewalk and another is driving in order to deliver a package from a truck.

We did not intend to be unfriendly nor dour though I can see (now) we have often and legitimately been so perceived. At one point in time I imagine we could not have been perceived any other way. Left by ourselves we did not know how else to be. We were made, mostly, all one way.

We, by Ourselves

We walk around puzzled for although we did not make ourselves we are left by ourselves. We have been given responsibility for ourselves in the very places, vast and difficult to avoid, over which those who made us exert control, both by nuanced suggestion and explicit design. Ambient and atmospheric interference has produced (and by atmospheric I do not mean the same thing as ambient, I mean heat turning into fire, radiation and floating dead animal bodies in the ocean water, infrared rays hitting hard on our faces and heads and chests, and nostrils overcoming the jet fuel, carbon monoxide, ozone, loud noises warning emergency or arrest) a formidable barricade, against which our ability to focus on each other gets lost or is absorbed, even when we are physically near as we most often are, pressed together by the *overcrowd*, a wide and nameless body of bodies or other kinds of energetic waves, that serves both as the intersection that conjoins us and the mass that prevents us. It is an impenetrable wall, or path or river, around and between us, which—and I'm of the strong opinion that this is unforeseen by those who'd made us and cleared these spaces for us but not *only* for us—provides foundation of our distinct moral and political formation.

In retrospect it sounds abstract but there was so much we did not know. There is still so much.

For example, we remain incapable of competition or unkindness, or kindness for that matter, in the case where kind implies human warmth emanating from an internal organ and glowing out of the eyes and mouth. There is nothing overtly abject about our material circumstance since we have been supplied the instruction and means for acting out a socially coherent notion of living as though we are Middle Class.

Gaps and Their Consequences

Our expressions, the laconic one and the one responsive to things, many things and every thing, did not read as contradictory. The huge spaces or dense blockades (*overcrowd*), which either contained things or not, made it difficult to reach and actually touch and makes this world in which we (still) find ourselves nearly impossible to capture—as it is and as it was—in our head, either all at once as unruly multiplicities and their desperately sought-after negations or as a distinct particular, a single absented thing once there and not yet.

For a time we continued to flounder in these gaps, trying to get out from under the (our) sea of stuff, reaching for these things neither there nor named. There, in the gaps, we first sensed that something wrong was being done to us.

Something, but not the thing.

By way of invention or reinvention, I don't know which, we began morning, sensing that morning left us closest to the plume of history and abundance from which we'd been evicted. Upon waking we danced together, all of us, sentient and being, our reaching and our touching issuing a violent impact upon the air and its imagined and imperceptible bodies and those that were actual and perceivable, moveable and changeable parts, shoulders, legs, breasts, hips, cheeks of ass and face, wrists—not rigid but rigidly inscribed to mean something about the person not persons to which it belonged. Each gesture was experienced like a blow which we were accustomed to receiving and so would feel that something was missing if it did not come, or did not come as a blow; this last a physical and psychic condition maliciously suggesting to us that we could not get so closely together, although we were formulating that very facility for intimacy as the unique contribution we'd make to alter our original design, the one made for us without us which imposed a standing and wicked pain we endured due to or despite the imposition of regularly sudden events—sirens which went off and to which we responded, dutifully, huddling, thrusting our bodies on top of each other, and the traffic jam that was metaphorically the same—a calculated assembly that banished morning's ardent tender ruptures and any feelings about all of it that could be left in us, those overflowing from inside us after dreams.

After and before we'd formulated this morning ritual, there were many sorts of conversations we knew how to have which were also brutal attempts that left us looking bruised and feeling like strangers to ourselves, as did our actions late in the day, outside, in the evenings, the heartbreaking and exhausting manner in which the many arms belonging to the group of us flailed though the air at riots and orgies, demonstrating our attempt to remember that day and the images amid which it glowered as it was beginning, because memory seemed to us a thread delicate and developing, which could become a durable and sturdy rope for we who were looking for a thing for why would we recall just a shadow a thing if it weren't at least a little bit true?

The Story of My Accident Is Ours

If I no longer exist, if in fact I may never have existed in the first place, then do I have a name? What is in a name?

We can ask these questions about such a name as Jane.

It was in my thinking about our names that I began to tell this story. It therefore follows to reason that thinking about names is the one true origin of my accident.

But I must account for the fact that my accident, which may have originated when it occurred to me that I did not know my name nor the name of any of us, came after the events of this story, which begins to be written when I begin to think this way about our names.

Before Origin

Names, by which we were called when we were called upon—
we were called upon often—operated as tags, verbal identifiers,
but not like signs. Signs, we are told, are mentally comprehensible
units that take on a discrete meaning in the mind, distinct from
the message the original represents. But the names we were called
conjured nothing except our conditioned response to being called
upon, most often for a task desired by another, requested from us,
and not infrequently as a means to clarify our presence at a job.

We were perfectly good at our jobs, which were not, after all,
demanding. Absolutely, we were bored. Our boredom at the job
did not particularly seem different than our boredom somewhere
else or in most of the other circumstances of our lives, defined
by vigilant reserve despite the giddy proliferation of stuff
with which they were filled to their tops, like buckets of rain,
following deluge.

Was it boredom?

As I write this, I find myself far from certain that what I am
describing—this tremendous aspect of our lives clamoring for

articulation, an all-consuming absence of affect in which we were left, such that the thing by which we were consumed and which made us always feel aware of the *threat* as both looming and happening at the same time was also something *foreign*, as a concept, outside immediate experience because we could neither apprehend nor comprehend it, leaving us in a situation in which we could only *pursue* it, for example, in movie theaters, where we went to press what was under our skin, and therefore sealed, through the surface, into a shared and public field of vision, assessment, objectification, tactile structure, something supra-organic, though having had once belonged to us, inside us, us lacking names, unnamable, untenable, adrift but not wandering—was not boredom after all but rather a constant state of seasickness in the way that seasickness implies the struggle of land leaving the body.

Land, which was once contoured and is now gelatinous.

Land, which exists and is by us missed.

(The Project)

(The Project) is very courageous. Some of us continue to do it and fail. To attempt it is to fail.

We have taken to an effort we call *our best*. Our best keeps us going with some degree of hope if not calm. It does not make us smug; it is merely that anxiety, when we do not do our best, threatens us with death—death physical and death real.

In death, we fail.

We try our best to make sense of death before anxiety kills. Then we try talking to it, then fighting with it, then pushing on it with all of our weight. Finally we do them all, knowing with each consecutive action that we are exactly where we started, and go back to doing it, from a new beginning, *the best* we can. Beginning there we appear innocent (animal) since it's impossible for us to *know* that we've been here before.

It is why we are called radical.

We can't know right away if we are able. We cultivate ethos that both holds us accountable and forgives us for our inability. There is a resignation about us, we watch revolutions carefully but cannot come up with anything fresh, anything that is not anticipated nor destroyed before we think of it.

We take comfort in the most predictable, unfettered human habits.

We reject the institutional.

It makes us *literally* itch.

Sight for Sore Eyes (The Project)

We wormed our way through the many iterations of how to act under the watchful eye of the State. The development of surveillance is by now understood by just about anyone so I do not need to describe it. Strange, how few would be able to describe it well with language though we all have a nearly physical understanding that the networks are pervasive and principled attempts at evasion pointless. We needed a new approach.

It was difficult to distinguish between new approach and renewed approach. Our powers to perceive slight distinctions were limited by the barren emotional state in which we had awoken to this world, an absence compounded biopsychosocially by being collectively encased by the State and its broad though seemingly *innocuous* apparatus, one that is in retrospect clever: blockades that were to the eye invisible and which created a slightly uncomfortable while predictable slapstick at least physical comedy experienced by us like those tricky mechanical doors that shut just as the body motions to go through; or regular and anticipated attacks by a crippling charley horse at every instance in which we positioned ourselves to rise into action after being still for too long, especially if what we'd intended or imagined were the sorts confrontational actions to which we aspired as a means to instigate the State to react and by doing so inadvertently release its or some of its secrets, and secret devices, and show us something we did not yet know, for we were developing a curiosity to know more about the world in which we found ourselves, despite being so conditioned, taunted as we were into terrible anxiety, by barricades and obstacles that were not simply so but deceptively so, held tightly and holding on tight by a confounding architectural fact: we were in structures clear as glass and apparently, open.

We have now come to recognize our pervasive and deep anxiety as some sort of emotion—I suspect in the canopy of fear—a particular quantity—not inverse to the depressive's fear of anxiety, not a fear of depression. Our brand of fear is caused by that which we are told we do not have and can never have and by our inability to make distinction between not having now and not possibly ever having.

We are so sucked out and scared we wear it like a fashion.

Rain brings it down a notch or two.

There is tremendous force in our make of fear. It is a fear so *great* it freezes us away from the things we love most, from the things we love to do, including fucking but far from limited to fucking.

Which is why we committed ourselves to (The Project).

We thought we would like to *make* something.

It is a terrible fear. We stall it when we can.

Public Space and Privasphere

I do not think that this world in which we found ourselves nameless, tagged, and more often than not allowed to physically survive, constitutes that thing which, before its obsolescence as a concept, was the thing thought of as *society* in the way that society implied a particular sort of non- or semi-commercial relationship which existed nearly but not quite squarely outside the operations of the State, with more of its weight being between and among its members, so as to be a thing simultaneously enforced upon us and generated from amongst us, a special contradiction of public and private invented by the then new ruling class before they were completely ruling and when they were installing, maneuvering and manufacturing improved conditions in which to be the ruling class, conditions which they advertised as being improved conditions for society, as a whole.

Unlike us, that infant ruling class of yesteryear, which is the mature ruling class presiding over the world in which we find ourselves, possessed and adamantly, defensively, eloquently, tactlessly and obsessively defined its *personality*, which they, as a class, thought of as something if not novel then incontrovertible, which they mannered as the public presentation of their desire which took the place of their desire, or so they proclaimed in confident yet demure display.

It came to be that this society of desire-masked-as-personality, which we, the adequately trained and prepared to live as the middle class, were to be seeking as our own personality and for which we were to deny ourselves our own desires and our own personalities, elided its very own self, and became, if not something new, a thing revealed through the ex post facto account of the past active discourse (i.e. hindsight), in which we who were certain we were supposed to be like that but didn't know why, and those who felt that because they understood why they *had* to be like that, were able to go on with our habit of fervent activity and not have a palpable impact on each other despite adjacency, proximity and other means of being close to a thing but not part of it.

It is in the fact that the once not-yet-completely ruling class had been able to be first the somewhat ruling class and later the ruling class completely that we learned—we could *see*—no, those of us who came before us could *see* and *come to know*, and therefore help us to see and come to know—that a something could come to be where something else was and furthermore that this replacing thing could shift and budge the shape of the rest of things until the shape of things was completely transformed into an exaggerated, or diminutive, or diminished version of the shape of the once new thing once it was no longer new.

Amid the vast and nearly completely unmanageable spaces between us, in the inarticulate detritus of their remainder, we found ourselves and found a place for ourselves—it had been as though we were on different banks of a deep, wide river which we wanted to cross and had been used to crossing before the bridges had been blown up to protect us so that in order to cross we would need to walk for miles along that same river to get to a bridge still standing and in doing so find ourselves in a dangerous confrontation *with* or in the employ *of* those who had come here to watch over us or those who *like us* happened upon those who had come here to watch over us and came to be in *their* employ and therefore be required to go after us. In these spaces we discovered that we belonged neither to the corporate body, nor to any of the small, more digestible parts from which it gained its most agreeable profit, nor to any anachronistic notion of a "society" at large, nor to any of the specific spheres which were thought to derive from this, *The Large*, always growing ever larger, as a whole.

The Large, as a Whole

In part, it was the obnoxious overload, that hungrily accruing pushiness (should I just say aggressivity?) of the *very very large* that pushed on us (yes aggressively) to picture a soft and glowing sphere, and the idea of *separate* sphere, as having so much promise that into this form-as-concept or concept-as-form we were willing to stake (The Project) in its *entirety*, including that small but *kinetic* bit of structuring (The Project) managed to gather toward navigating the liquid voids of our world.

We *pictured* (and failed to sufficiently *articulate*) the sphere as an object emanating beneficence, something touchable, into which we could walk and perhaps inhabit, a solid which nonetheless had a property that enabled it to react with and neatly dissolve so many of the rough particles of our days, and also as the infinite we might control, a singular vehicle for emancipation from all the terrible requirements being manufactured and churning out from the *large*, demands which were accumulating in us as they were building rapidly, isometrically, and exponentially in front of us.

Our strategy was later revealed as naïve, but not *completely* naïve.

Nor was it, our strategy, *ironic*, in manner, mood or tone, *irony* being the sort of thing at which we were clumsy, if not completely powerless to conjure, let alone perform, as a social act.

Therefore, it was not irony; it was rather *coincidence*, that can explain the fact of our timing: strategizing around spheres at the same time of…no, in anticipation of a *disastrous turn* for which, due to our simultaneous vows and commitments, we were put in the position, *required to be in the position*, to serve as both *culprit* and *witness* for the pervasive shockwaves and viral proliferation that produced multiple and unanticipated epidemics: a total catastrophe of *sphere spawning*. Suddenly, there were lots and lots of them and lots of kinds of them, some shapely, some transparent, others hidden underground with protective devices pointing upward aboveground, and ones made of tinted glass, occupying space in the middle of the street, often identified by the neighbors and beat(ing) cops as unsanctionably *loud*.

Loudest are those hovering just *above* the rest of us, surveilling as they always must (these not only categorically spheres but *qualitatively* spheric), chasing all of us into uninvited and awkward contact with each other so that we in the spheres underground with devices pointing were contortioned to be improperly, uncomfortably *viewing* that which was going on in the ones that are tinted, loud, taking up some *small* but *contested* spot in the middle of the blacktop.

Less appealing, though seemingly more *comfortable*, are the patched green spheres, but these hazard the constant irritant of flies flying around our faces. Although frequent, generally the manner by which flies land, upon foreheads and noses is momentary, indelicately light, which denies us the time required to grow accustomed to the sensation of them landing there. Within the green we are equally gravely disturbed by allergies that itch and irritate our eyes and nostrils, and ants that crawl over the cheeks of our asses and into our thighs and crotch, so that although the thick renovated lawn looks inviting, what we experience is a *mean and red* burning and scratching of our most sensitive areas that despite *our best* effort and determined optimism, we find ourselves *perfectly* unable to relax.

Spheres that are spacious, beautiful, ergonomically designed, protected, and covered in white, are generally less disturbed by the constant irritant of invasive blue force than our dark glass and metal spheres (whose interiors were constructed of animal skins and wood pieces, recovered by expert and now long dead underwater divers on dangerous missions into large and surprisingly well-preserved ships that had sunk long long ago in frightfully frigid waters, waters so cold they are *even colder than the temperature of freezing* and then molded by trained and weathered hands into a convex shape, which, we might say in this context, manifested an inverted sphere).

Although more *protected* and cost prohibitive, these white spheres, inhabited by mostly elegant bodies, have windows so clear and clean they are also, perhaps counter-intuitively to the naked eye, the most easily apparent or transparent spheres and so experience another version of being pointed to and shot at, an affliction which often precipitates for the manicured, sleek bodies within a humiliating public dip into the state penitentiary, or, when they are lucky, the local jail, so that in part they share the restricted and guarded living toward dying that was inflicted upon so many of us less shiny and seen, then and still on this uncannily radiant day.

Such conflation of types and sorts traumatized we who'd tried to keep track of it all because we'd marked the making of spheres as a tactic or strategy (from this vantage point I can't decide which it is) for building a space where we thought we would be able to maneuver and begin to practice our movement of liberation, or, our *next* movement of liberation.

Apparently, before us and among us, there have been others.

Only now can we comprehend spheres as a central component of the large aggressive campaign for the internment of all space. Spheres were and in fact still are everywhere and nowhere exactly in the public sphere which can no longer be, nor breathe, now that its surface has been covered and its air filled by the desperate, manic, birthing of spheres everywhere, everywhere apparent and less apparent, which also makes for us an increasingly populated world.

Opening Action (The Project)

Our first action (The Project) was to examine the world from every angle.

We were discomfited by the notion of blind spots. We burrowed into vigil against danger and toward the yet to be discovered element which might scientifically provide us the means to reverse and repair the wrong being done to us.

Previous turns at revolution had suggested a science so advanced as to be unlimited by science and therefore capable of presenting something true, though momentary. We liked the momentary; it provided us the rare breaks we took from responsibility. We tried to see the world from every angle. We did not think this meant we were in charge.

To look at the world from any angle means that we believe it to be true; we are universally submerged into the deepest, darkest depth of a spectacle of consumption. Repeatedly and tirelessly, in one gallant effort after another, we tried to shake it, to rise from under its toxic, plastic weight, until we could no longer deny our discovery that it was nearly impossible to not be thus submerged so long as we were ourselves in the world in which we found ourselves, and furthermore that it would be terrible to not be that way since to not be that way would mean making enemies with those we would need to have as friends.

This is why we go to the movies.

In the movies we watch evidence that we are extremely strong—and palpable. In the movies we achieve superhuman bodies (hearts) in addition to superhuman brains. We see that humor must be grand, for we observe how an *idea* is taken and stretched into visual impunity made reproducible, pliable enough to last the correct duration.

This was then, there. But what about here, where it begins. With Baudrillard? Benamin? With Bataille. Most certainly it begins with Bataille. For it was he who saved (The Project) for this later date.

Whether (The Project) is good and necessary, if saving it provides something good or helpful in the gaps where once stood a society and before stood something else, I cannot say. Nor is this a particularly central problem to the story of my accident.

On the *other* hand, I do want to know.

Perhaps all of us do…

Was it true? Our spooky sense that a *helping* hand was held out to us there in the dark, and that our Vigil Against Harm was simultaneously a grab for it, and that this *hand*, which teased us with aid but also *threatened* us with the very harm that we were trying so hard and blindly to avoid, was there and there particularly for us—*we* who came into this world all at once and all one way?

Which way was it?

Unquiet to not know and sit quiet not knowing, we started crawling, sometimes carefully and sometimes spasmodically, without clue to which direction or to what end but, despite the taciturn look in our face and the speed we seemed to lack, not purposelessly, for we were a far cry and kept ourselves a fair distance from those beings who'd be described as being without a purpose.

On the contrary, it was in these movements that we began to seek the names we sought from outside of ourselves, we who until then, though aware of ourselves as selves, remained remarkably nameless.

Happiness

Expressionlessness and boredom do little to betray the energy of the work demanded of us by a difficult navigation of signs, a cacophonous multitude pointing toward us and into every direction around us, composed of straight lines jutting into the projectile points of two line-drawn arrows, or of shaded and curved and crooked trajectories gathering into dimensional representations of a nasty long boney index finger—a witch's hooking gesture. Both in their own way were ominous enough to suggest unspeakable punishment if we did not obey their crisscrossed instructions to traverse narrowly, or was it circuitously, along paths poised to suggest a multiplicity but which would then authoritatively combine us and the variety of paths on which we'd begun multiply, seemingly randomly, even dreamily, into one *definitively* singular march.

Beyond and in addition to the demands of the ubiquitous rebus of these tangled two- and three-dimensional surfaces disguised as helpful state infrastructures and technological convenience, was yet another demanding super-structural shove, so strong and everywhere that it was like gravitational force, into the discovery, production and distribution of *happiness.*

According to Aristotle evil is opposed to evil. Our greatest oppositions originate from the forms with which they are most alike. Happiness was far from the only word-entity that was used in phenomenologically diverse manners by people who spoke the same language and were in the same room. Some words were themselves defined so in the glossary, to mean both themselves and their opposites, or near opposites.

We were alarmed by such words, so collected them. Some of the most disturbing remain on our list as words we find ourselves unwilling to circumnavigate without: address, against, beauty, bolt, cleave, disintimate, gift, girlfriend, incorporate, infamous, let, mean, moot, object, oversee, project, rap, ravel, root, sanction, strike, weather, and many others, including foreign words like *gehenstadt*, or *heimlich and unheimlich*, which you can read more about in the chapter, "The Story Around My Accident."

Like the sphere epidemic—coincidentally or not—the happiness problem arrived at the critical climax of our becoming (The Project), during which we began to experience ourselves as cohesive, and better still, in possession of, a concentrated intent on action and activity. In other words, at the very moment within which we were beginning to *stir*, or *stir things up*, the State in all its earnestness and productivity, having become gravely concerned that the erasures and the subsequent evenness was producing a massive and profit-crippling ennui among its people, initiated the release of a Happiness campaign whose earmark was an omnipresent billboard that read "Happiness for all beings." At first these signs read "Happiness for all people, no matter color, class nor creed." Besides the obvious troubles with the poetry of the phrase—which issued from a well-intentioned but misguided desire to articulate its revolutionary, progressive and democratic commitments (its election campaign slogan had been: "All things to all people"), there were complaints. The Spiritualists who, to our surprise, had become a tightly organized activist force in our time, launched their own campaign by way of constant media of every sort, at all hours, every day (their numbers were by this time vast), to merely change the phrasing slightly so that beyond the limitation set by the word "people" the slogan would include all things. For they, the Spiritualists, understood as we did that language has meaning. Thus a slight change in the wording of this governmental campaign could move people's consciousness, could in fact be radical even in its own religious right. A change in the phrasing such, by this slight edit, would mean shifting orientation from a state advertisement that amounted to something like happiness propaganda to a polite request to consider a different notion of consciousness. And though we were a bit mocking of the Spiritualists for their funny science, we were impressed by this coup, that without a levy, they had essentially gotten the State to do their bidding.

Some of us, alcoholics and suicides, were so impressed we made an attempt to join the Spiritualists ourselves, logically reasoning this could, for us 'kill two birds with one stone,' and knew better than to repeat this idiom in the presence of our new community, which espoused a reverence for all beings and would find such lackadaisical and cruel language behavior, if not irredeemable, something which would require a corrective treatment, or, to put it less disruptedly and into a language habit of the Spiritualists themselves, it provided 'a win-win situation;' not only were they effective politically, their program suggested interruption against the exact vulnerabilities we feared we were most subject to, us as alcoholics, us as suicides, and us as the rest.

It didn't work. It *wasn't* the very same vulnerabilities among them and us all. The happiness the Spiritualists offered made us feel lethargic and dumb, which was the very situation we'd been trying our whole lives living in this world to diagnose and if not cure, at least improve with dialogue and great attempts toward the invention of difference, derived from our pained longing for a change of some sort, the possibility of which seems to defy logic, for how could we become other than as we were, especially since we were, following the design planned by both us and them, all one way. But it persisted in us, the notion that if we made heroic effort, and stayed the course (which course would it be?), and cared a very great deal about it, then at least an incremental alteration might build us, and the world in which we found ourselves; and that would be enough, all that were necessary, however little it'd be.

Mischievous Traces

Our uncanny confidence in the revolutionary result of a slight shift in the possibilities of our world created both a common space and a sharp division between us and most of the other sorts milling about in our times, including those on the television with broad, radiating smiles. Of all the sorts and possible sorts we encountered in our world, it was our closeness to the Spiritualists we found most unsettling, so much so that because of it, as a direct result of it, we went forward into our world with a sense of doubt which also followed us closely from behind and so was right there upon us when we were suddenly stopped, as they say, dead in our tracks, though at this point in our story only metaphorically dead and for all intents and purposes, we could have, I mean that we had the physical ability to, continue in another direction, either back or to the left, and that is what we did, but individually, for the path of each was distinct once the one path we'd agreed upon was thusly abruptly disturbed. Beyond their sly efficacy, collective speech habits and physically-etched code of discipline, it was they, the Spiritualists, who found comfort in that which we found most frightening; that thing, which is a thing so slickened by profuse overuse I find it difficult to stay with the thought of it over the duration required by writing but may posit at least certain defining negatives for the time being: this thing for them and for us both was not fame nor passivity, not prayer nor the mean profiteering war mongering broadcast everywhere, none of which are exactly the same thing as, but all of which are well connected to, the glimmering smiles on television.

Furthermore, and this complicates it and makes it more slippery still, this element that we shared with the Spiritualists was just as central to them in their ideas as it was to us in ours, though it led them and us to resulting conclusions which are most definitely and diametrically opposed. Were the costs not as high and our convictions not so steady, would I feel less tortured while writing this? Perhaps not, but how could they be otherwise? For of all the aspects of life for which my accident may have provided some sort of perspective, hindsight of happenings and their causes and consequences, toward this difficulty in particular, it offers nothing.

We stay the course (whichever course), believing as we did then— I did say believing, I haven't yet formulated the exact language— that although the slight alteration and the infinitesimal space that course makes is both the place of possibility and the place of the unknown. We understood it as merely that which we ourselves took responsibility for and they, the Spiritualists, well, I am far from a reliable witness, but it was for them that exuberant belief called faith, in 'higher' or 'infinite' power, which could rob me of my ability to sleep at night, if I had the ability to sleep at night.

Evidence or Sign

It seems needless to say we did not believe in miracles nor care so much about alien occurrences, even as they affected us. They profoundly affected us. We were especially sensitive to loud noise and random violence perpetrated by the State on unprotected urban bodies because they were or we imagined them to be our bodies. The sudden and specific military or police helicopters, the magical anticipation suggested by the blue or steel barricades that appeared every time we joined each other in a social group on the street, the scuffles, the injuries resulting in neck braces, the rain of charged projectiles aimed into our fleshy sides and boney middles—these were the dependable features in our lives toward which we'd grown expectant, not only but *especially* when we did not express our appreciation about the armed and dominating presence in our midst, customary and alien, and the blurring of the vision we thought we *required* for our nervous, hazy pursuit.

Indeed, we often perceived things that *looked like* evidence of the increment we sought but in moments that pass as quickly as they reveal themselves, like turning our heads to confirm to ourselves that what we saw was a little girl on the sidewalk gliding past us *two feet above the ground* without the aid of a machine…by the time we see her face-to-face she is back on the ground smiling at us and all we have for a fact is that of our confidence or its lack.

These moments pass quickly and because of this very fleeting aspect, don't hold up well, if at all, in the telling. How one knows or thinks we are attending such a window in time and space does itself feel somewhere between impression and intuition, both are suspicious even to we who like such things and are prone to resist the chill of scientific inquiry. Although I do feel strongly that being able to give images toward this thread would help, I find that when I reach for one I am back to relying on the categories which such revelatory moments of incremental alteration transcend, for it is not that men are not acting like men, nor the rich or famous bearing no affect of reflected projection, but rather that one witnesses an opening in which the terms are expired into the dust they were born to become, when the accumulated anxieties of past experience melt because the stern-looking teacher posted firmly besides us making us more than a little nervous with impressive stature emanating from macho bearing and muscular heft asks, before explaining to us that which we don't yet know, but need to know in order to complete the task to which we've been assigned, "Tell me first, how might I help you best?

Nothing Doing (The Project)

Because the world makes us lethargic and dumb, and because the world that makes us lethargic and dumb outrageously demands our focus on *doing* things, doing things all day long and long into and all the way through the night too, rather than *seeing* things, we agreed that better than to do something is to make something.

In a long moment of *continuous*, meaning not yet effectively or clumsily resisted, somnambulism, we considered naming our project (The Project) of Doing, when the calamity of that close call woke us *up* in the middle of our dreaming walk-sleep *stumbling* upon scorn, horror and dismay over that half of the verb's meaning (*facere*).

For the world, which makes us lethargic and dumb *does* so by a manner of exhaustion; we are thus vacant or delirious, lost beyond that most firm pedosphere somewhere real and beneath us, to which we must return, either *just in time* or *not at all*, to face each other with clear unobstructed sight, in order to stop doing it, and start making it.

Relieved by the closeness of the call more accurately the nearness of that fall we *vowed* to impose a structural, lexical and syntactic program of material *intention*. (For a longer treatment of 'intention' see chapter "All Intentions are Good.") Looking back on this, I do not think we knew the enormity of such a task, the risk involved in our really making a thing. Beyond the facts of plastic, latex, fiberglass, heavy and not so heavy metals and all the spatial contingencies of matter, there were unforeseen necessary consequences to introducing new form into the world.

But we were hell-bent.

And we were afraid.

We are still afraid.

We, as Selves

In retrospect this brings up the question of whether or not we were clear of our intentions inside our most singular selves or if the formulation we'd constructed around the group of us imploded when alone in our bed at night our minds traveled the landscape of the completed day and its treacheries, examining a newly visible (articulated) pitfall or two (which rise up, although represented here as recessive declines) in the strategic thinking of (The Project) of Making which we would the next day rejoin, bursting with *vigor* (a revelation in and of itself) and *steely* determination to present to the public our confidence that (The Project) of Making was yes necessary and our position was *good* and *right*, no. Better, no. It was undoubtedly *best*.

(Several chapters that follow, including "(The Project) of Making," "Second Happiness" and "Love Everyone" expand upon these "pitfalls in the strategic thinking.")

Although we did not and determined that we could not *properly* define ourselves, we'd concocted an imperious air, in part because the alternative, our look of unknowing, appeared incorrectly as a refusal to know and in part because we were gesturing toward making ourselves now of *our own* design. We needed to appear, amongst ourselves, in the mirror and as presentation piece to the world in which we found ourselves, *directed* while at the same time thinking about such foreign and abstracted things as the *future*. We'd concluded the future belongs to those who envision or imprison it. We came to consider that perhaps we should not shy away…might not we attempt to contribute a future less poisonous, atomized, wasting and ruined for the world into which surely others will find themselves awakening like us, shouldering unknown traits and ways. There was an inherent danger in this idea for we were a body systematically denied the images and sensory input necessary to build an imagination fertile enough to grow a vision for modeling, there was so little of the stuff that marks itself unknown. One day one of us enthusiastically talked about 'the good mess to be in' and a pall of dumbfounded confusion fell over the group. It seemed meaningless yet took up all the space in the tight urban room.

We stand our ground, with fragility but not meekness, refusing the hurled critique. Lacking ego to begin with, *ego* does not present as obstacle but always *vacancy*, the very air we breathe, the *breach* between the world so very flattened and the world that could not yet exist, a breach completely *unscalable* without the aid of those helpful, inscrutable and desirous hands, transparent and lacking transparency, a most beautiful kind foe that did not disdain us for our barren condition, blank countenance, erratic gestures and guttural sounds.

Sensing the risk, we imagined an alternative which was surely worse, to not anticipate the new and future world, and will it to unforeseen hungry victors, random as they would be, mutant evolutions notable for their strange and most unpleasant capacity to be envious of that which is yet to be.

And are there not things, the profitability of which, despite being calculated in advance of their occurrence by the formulations of power into which so much collective energy has been consumed for refining that still do manage to become themselves? Am I talking about Spirit, or Personality or Destiny when I say this? I tend to think here the exact term matters less than a little girl, killed in front of us after only 20 seconds, or the brute who can't help from taking all, or the one who fattens then flattens then all together disappears. Though the force of Profit is far from meaningless it operated as that, a force. Like many though not all forces, its nature is to obliterate opposing force. But who could ever believe in a physical world with only one to weigh us down?

You see how I go on. Despite my accident, and its long history and complex antecedents, I remain afraid still but do continue. Anyway, it's beautiful, clear and cold today. The image is nearly complete.

Second Happiness: Quake

Confined to one institutional room, held there under careful scrutiny by a team of bulky guards, trained watchers wearing unmistakable at the same time inconsistent trained watcher garb, on their unmistakable at the same time distinctly irregular frames, who were nonetheless uniform in a performance of insistent gesticulation and firm assertion that we must sit still in the chairs they provided, chairs as sturdy as they were stiff, structures not unlike the sorts of peoples Gulliver encounters, tiny or gigantic or positioned in so strange a direction that no matter our selection, small, medium or large, we find our legs dangling, or our knees pressing to bend so deeply they point like the sharp arrow drawn horizontally by two right angulated lines, or the nearly bare bones of our bottom pushes harshly into the hard back of the chair, or the fleshy soft there overflows the boundaries, impaled by sharp sides paling from a loss of blood flowing within, so that we ache when we make an effort to fold our legs and sit straight up where anyway we find ourselves sideways, or high and above, or low and below.

Such discomforts disarrange, prohibiting somatic and kinesthetic transfer at the precise moment in which each of us encounters the unfamiliar stir, as vibration that passes through us and along the contour of us, trying to move from one body to the next as received communication, a charge sometimes met, moved along by another just behind it and one just in front, against statistical odds but possible in spite of the derangement, and much more often, because of it, left hanging there at the limit of the body, its line severed, its correct conduct cut short.

Although its nature is motion, it lingers in a room saturated with it.

We were in jail when we first acknowledged, by saying or thinking— as ever it is difficult to make this distinction except in retrospect when the fact of it as something which did *indeed happen* despite any lack of material trace left behind comes out more *evidently* in the telling than in the mere thinking—something about us shifted and we were afterwards undeniably different.

I do *believe* it happened to all of us equally and all at once as a quake even though there were only mere physical signs of this: a flash of brightness in our eyes and static exciting the thick and thin hairs covering our bodies, particularly those standing up on the backs of our necks, all movements of impact which are nonetheless practically imperceptible to any observer. They were at the same time impossible to actually ignore so that even our (once) spongy guards, who'd been taught to resist our bodies (a key component of their job training was comprised of a series of simulations designed to build into them an immunity against sympathetic gestures and vulnerable tremors that would normally evoke from the watcher the impulse to help) were once again made subject to (or were they objectified by?) a faint but *inescapable* perception (flies, landing lightly and momentarily) and so became immediately more alert and suspicious of us in that tiny window, which we knew very well away from which we must yank our heads and bodies, so we could not be viewed, although that yank itself was yet another *too quick* movement, which had the consequence of disenabling us from leaving a deposit, either for recall shortly later or for researched reconstitution in some far off time we cannot conceive of here yet, in the telling, or there then, in the happening.

I say that I believe, and perhaps we all did believe, but, because of the disarray, the saturation, the fact that it happened under the sign of the absent mark, unimpressed upon airy oral and tidy textual surfaces, I cannot *know* for sure whether it indeed happened to each of us equally and all the same way.

We can however finally say *for certain* because of it existing *now* in written form, that we all think that it was a thing *thought* and *only thought* (no one recalls hearing anything, no words were extracted in the questioning) and that this *in retrospect* is a good thing.

Second Happiness: Penthouse

By way of spoken or written reports requested by us from each of us individually (we were thorough, we did not remove ourselves from the scientific methods of our times) it does now appear— for this was the information that emerged (and what did not, despite the facility's refined eye and motion sensitive cameras) from interviews and video (rocking gesticulations that too failed to exist) we learned that we were thinking and perceiving *simultaneously* during the *thing* or 'infragle,'[1] —a word which did eventually congeal on the surface for general use to indicate this *sort* of thing, although it had not yet emerged right then. The event itself came to be called *Wrinkle* (for among its other effects, it aged us) or, more colloquially amongst we who were *there* then, *Penthouse* (the name of our elevated cell) and was widely respected as indicative proof that we were making progress in our efforts at understanding our world by being more intimately a part of our world whether it wants us or not.

---

1 INFRAGLE—*noun* \in-'frā-gəl, -(,)'fre-\—undetectable yet cataclysmic shift in sensate perception or knowledge.

We choose to continue, to suffer and remain entwined in the brambles of this world in which we find ourselves—so uncompromising in its ambivalence, carelessness and even hostility toward us, which here says nothing about the guarded, concave, hesitant posture we wear in this world in order to be able to face it, full on and frontally.

Second Happiness: Trace

In times of intense desire but poor recognition we find ourselves least formed by language, most likely and with all our effort producing merely a grunt or two, or a grunt and a hum and a gesture, if we are lucky. We did not like the grunting sounds nor the shared experience resulting out of them although we secretly and hopefully understood them to be only transitional regressions, depressions of language in which language subjects itself to being turned over and tilled or drilled, making itself temporarily unavailable, and that on the other side of it there'd be a chance for a renewed spirit of words. This secret belief emboldened us to refuse the clamoring assertions of our defeat.

The other times we found ourselves unable to produce anything but a grunt were those when we were confronted by inescapable opposition, as such we found ourselves at the moment of my accident.

Still for us a certain excitement accompanies these moments— the one in the jail was the first of several—excitement both over the fact that something is happening and that we can be confident that something is happening, because although about which emotion we were having we could not be absolutely sure, we were at least almost sure that an emotion had in fact occurred or was in fact occurring. Some of these (can I call them feelings?) were more fleeting than others (I prefer not to call them feelings). Most were at first overwhelming, completely *circuit blowing* phenomena and therefore difficult to simply label, as for example 'happy' but we could not imagine that such exuberance could indicate 'sad'.

Without map, dictionary or guide, we were on the lookout for other emotions, a range, suspecting that like gender, the endless possibilities were culturally and linguistically constricted only by the interests of power, which seeks linearity and simplicity though it cannot actually be so or have it so, or have it be so. As one can tell from the bewildered expressions on faces when complexity is revealed, these polarities dominate the emotional field and most often prevail so that we would nearly universally agree on any particular face, to which side it belongs.

Take for example a smirk.

Whether or not it is distinct from a shit-eating grin.

Distraction

Impotent to change the times we were in or to depart from them for a spell or for a while, we continue to take them in, observing and figuring this world in which we find ourselves. We don't imagine this is a worse world than any other, although that notion was being implied socially and expressed medially with regularity and emphasis. The way in which it was regularly and emphatically expressed was presented formally, as art or scholarly study, worthy of the significant investment of energies spent in its service. I could not help but notice that for all the creative and intellectual fervor poured into the expressions of our times, we were mostly being told things that we already knew, things so repeated and obvious, the teller of these things *had* to know that we already knew.

We suppose they know what they are doing when they tell these things which are already known and which we know they know we already know and which we don't *only* already know—but which we know *as do they* that we have been told them *many times* before and will be told, if all goes according to their plan, *many times* again.

This aspect of the means by which our world was represented and reported to us made it all the more difficult, upon discovering our emotions, to stop thinking about the emotions—for they were thus far, unrepresented, unsignaled by noisy broadcast or pictorial or textual signage. We began to look toward the emotions, more and more, and less at the visual evidence of the world, from every angle. Neither did *this* make us feel we were in charge, though perhaps it made us more attuned to the rupture in which our bodies were formed and in which we have labored for them to continue to form.

Rigid Bodies

The body we wore when we came into the world in which we found ourselves was not our body and we did not know its ways. Some of us were sensitive to noise and some of us were easily stimulated by sex. Some of us liked to dress like smiling people on television. Some of us followed lovers around and some of us waited for lovers to come. Some of us wanted to be touched only one way and some of us found pleasure in being touched all kinds of ways. Some of us switched back and forth and some of us stayed the same. Some found it painful to be one way but not another; some found it painful to be any other way; some found pain to be the case any way at all.

In the times of which I speak in the world into which we woke, the State, committed to all people and to all things, *enabled*, in the manner of removing roadblocks, loosening safety regulations and forgiving discouraging tariffs, the research and corporate development of a variegated technology, a not very neatly packaged popular science, that allowed bodies and their parts to change and interchange. In this we began to witness a veritable *mechanics* for the animal body, outfitted into so many easily procured consumables. More still, the State made *ecstatic* way for the industry and its products, *lubricating* pipes, *opening* ports, *stimulating* sales. The technology thus *encouraged*, we watched it sail easily along otherwise static packed channels that branched out to a complicated and oft unanticipated grid which had before our times been expanded and now reached into each and every crevice, gaudily lit by enormously tall aluminum orbs, permissively read from above by thundering satellites, electronically measured from below. Chaotically wrapped or convincingly boxed or left out naked and raw, dividing and subdividing away from conglomerated mass beginnings into a multiple, many tiered, in itty bitty and chunky parts, mixed scale system; and trading in pieces sized unevenly, big, medium, small, and value pack; and sorts, prize-winning, genetically modified, state-of-the-art, economy, deluxe, exclusive, naturally derived, certifiably organic. Each size and sort is allowed to randomly find its way into a well-suited locale, insuring every class of population a security of supply, efficiently delivered in terms of speed, if not quality or safety, like so many other combustible goods that tumble into the markets of our world.

Thus, body mechanics became available for purchase in every sphere—for elegant fortunate bodies that is, and for we generally less so there were back alleys, corner stores and country borders. Word of available modification was spread by advertisement on trains and by show and tell in what was left of unpoliced dark corners (park) before the rising of an unfriendly, invasive sun. Future consumers were made less strange to the fluids and blood and guts of it by graphic and moving pictures on television and live demonstrations at the club.

The world, in which had once stood a society and now stood something else, had accommodated and absorbed these technologies quickly, but was not able to do this so very peacefully when it came to certain classes of bodies, certain body types and certain exchanges. Inversions of hormones, genitals and vocal cords, generated a rabid violence onto the death by the practitioners and purchasers of upgrades to skin, hair, chin and breasts, and from those who had gone by a *swallow* from scrawny to buff, or by a *pinch* from fat to thin.

What I am describing refers directly to the beginning of the story when I said one could not oppose this thing. To oppose these mechanics, their divisions and tangled convolutes of distribution, would mean being against ourselves as a people who consumed and needed to consume as a means of living in this world, managing our suffering as a thing ever attached to the *body* of our life like an abandoned starving nursing child, who belongs to us and whom we love as though we could love ourselves. Absolute or even partial refusal on ideological grounds would implicate us as being unmoved by our very own suffering. Which we are not.

The Movies, Free with Killing

I appreciate the way that in the movies free with killing, death takes on a different logic.

We were unmoored, but not unmoved. We empathized…with the possible future life of a little girl appearing for 20 seconds in a film.

If everyone in her life is killed in front of her, we won't mind so much the noise she makes that will lead the killers to killing her as well.

We refuse to be turned away by the stench, the overrun of visible mildew, the wear, the gold embossing, and red, purple, blue velvet or velour upholstery upon which yes, we are uncomfortable, alternating our weight from one sore, sweaty butt bone to the other on the no longer cushiony surface.

We, front-lit, back to the dark, learning about things onto which we held or tried to hold, tightly and ineffectually, as they passed off-screen into our effort to make them real, practicing the motions on the inside.

We, together, in wide, flesh-torn seats, thinking together, that the alternative, holding onto the course of her life alone and always with this blood before her eyes, is certainly worse.

We are born of an abstraction, we are not made uncomfortable by the idea of where we end and our abstraction begins.

And yet we are not yet made of abstraction. Not, and not entirely.

Therefore, I can assure you that when I speak of death I am speaking of actual death, neither abstract nor metaphorical.

My Death

I, of course, saw my death before I died, though by then it is true, I could not stop it, I'd already walked into the accident knowingly but, by the time it was about to happen, I and the others had fully and completely set our course; there was no outcome other than my death.

Accident

The sun is out in the morning, after a night of listening to rain hitting the roof above.

It doesn't matter, every scene of the accident must be recalled over and over again ad infinitum because its revelations are slow and endless, each one leading to less thinking than the one before. Not thinking does nothing and makes for no difference in the story, which begins with thinking correctly and acting exactly the same as if our actions had been innocent.

We walk into the accident knowing it will happen.

To look at uncertainty from another angle, one might feel shame. But we are innocent. The only method we had for avoiding my accident was offered by those who had made us. Who had made such a long and hollow space for us.

There is a vividness to any fall, an intensity of its totality; no inhalation, no fast sex, no whack to gain power or money, no ideology, no pleasurable purchase, no fragrant food, not even the stroke on the cheek will address.

Perhaps the stroke on the cheek. More as concept than as sensation.

There are consequences to my death, to being on the other side also the same side and not the outside. I see things either less clearly or with less depth and no longer experience the cinematographic viewing I recall now as memory, in which the city itself takes on the timing of a reel of film.

There was music and the music did a thing.
Someone came and made it stop.

A repressed or discarded urge.
Light footing near the static-filled canal.

All Intentions Are Good

I didn't miss, still cannot miss, the previous, though I remember
it in full sensory detail. Delicate limbs,
especially wrist.

Our sadness now unlike before causes us to feel that we ourselves
are the wrong being done to us, and cannot think of any other way.

We can no longer say.
What we meant, the complicated wellness of our intent.

The Story Around My Accident

I often wonder what was it that drove me, and by me, I want to explain, *someone like me*, toward that imminent disaster, for I am neither self-destructive nor suicidal. Most of us were neither of those things. Occasionally, one postures, urged on by the loneliness, but even we who do, fools as we are, can soon acknowledge the error in our ways, one born of misreading our loneliness, which most often results in our deep embarrassment over our behavior that was caused by said confusion. Obvious, this last comment, and this next: that another common distraction was drink, perhaps even more common and oblivious than the false suicides. Us drinkers became tedious—in part because by the century's definitions we would enter program. Program was a useful tool, but like the others offered up to us an empty one. We were incapable of lightness. Language and laughter, stories from worlds we hadn't been born into, all of which we needed to formulate an alternative response to our addiction, were out there, but not programmatically; there was a huge gap between ourselves and the world in which we found ourselves to which we felt a terrible responsibility but could not easily enjoy.

Still, it wasn't an impulse toward suicide or self-destruction that led me to my accident. I should say "The Accident" because officially, it is not mine alone. I have come to think of it rather as disorientation. Not of sexual disorientation, or sexual orientation, for that matter, because like the German 'heimlich' and 'unheimlich', and the English 'ravel' and 'unravel' those are more alike than opposite. For to be overly sexually orientated was understood as a repressed disorientation, or the opposite, I cannot remember. Either way, on this issue, which was a popular centerpiece of conversation in our time, we were well-balanced or disoriented, it is hard to say which.

articulated and most silenced—that occasionally a star possessing brilliance enough to be able to operate all the cultural and class systems at once does come along and this star has the force to cause the whole thing (on its very own terms) to rumble, at least quiver. Such a rattling has at times produced an amnesty in which doors open and a few others of us are able to rush in, or out, but for most of us, there is an ever denser charge—an injunction to buy our way out of our predicament by signing onto an ideology the best of us oppose vehemently and toward which the worst of us are ambivalent. We are led to believe and we convince ourselves this point of purchase is some minor detail, that if we know we don't mean what we say then it will not materialize—although here we fidget more restlessly even than our usual, we shuffle where we stand, nervous, suspecting, nearly knowing what we already do— that speech and knowledge are convolutes and cannot be any other way, that words, spoken or written, make it matter—each one having some sort of impact if not 'meaning' so to speak, despite ambiguity, complexity, politesse, magic tricks, good humor and the weather. Black, White and Left, Right can each mean many things so we are warned to not define these things narrowly or generally, to be particularly conscious when using these apparently basic even banal words for wouldn't we all agree, black is a word that means dark and white a word that means light and that dark is understood to be under, feared like a basement or as a place to hide, as within a thick forest or under a blanket, and light is received as a place of hope and exposure, levity and wisp.

Furthermore those narratives had been insisted upon by histories doubly violent first in their enactment, again in their interminable retelling through which our limited knowledge of the emotions has been maintained.

We like to believe we can relax from all of it, the State, the histories, the enforced purchased means of survival, vigilance in language, and to trust those amongst whom we find ourselves, the warm, loving and bohemian neighbors that have moved in across the hall, and those with whom we share our work on (The Project). But, by shattering what illogical, inexplicable confidence we had, The Accident has made it even more impossible to know which way we walk or if we walk at all upon the earth below us or if there is in fact an earth or a below upon which we might now walk.

Many years ago I saw a film that led me to think about the one moment of my life that I would like to keep forever after my death. Although isolating a single representative moment was a false practice, it was not difficult.

The moment consists of two together among many in the background. It is neither a movie, nor a photo.

It could be on the television. As a commercial whose product is uncertain.

I pick up a book. I open the Internet. I like the authors. They are women. I go look for a man. I remember that now there is no man is no woman.

Only we who.

I think of we and seek some comfort, something sure, something that will let me know which way, back or forth.

I should choose today.

I write a letter. It is electronic.

I open the door. I can't breathe. I close the door. I think about breathing about where it begins and how far it can go. I'm nervous. I'm anxious. I'm mad.

I'm nervous I'm anxious I'm mad and I can't really breathe. I go out the door. I take a phone call, outside the door. It's him. I can't find us anywhere. He gives me instructions. I follow them. Everything he says sounds wrong. I say nothing. I follow the plan. There is no plan. The plan is written as its events occur.

After Image

The ground beneath us cannot be trusted; we need new ground. There is a history of art that is well known to us in our times, of found objects reconfigured because although the past is nearly universally understood to be destructive as a force left to itself we find it impossible to retire. Rather than wrestle with its unruly enormity, we resign ourselves to picking up its pieces, though often, we throw them right back down.

Some, those we consider visionaries, collect these ejected pieces off city streets in order to rearrange them into small monuments which become passing moments for passersby who wait with uncertainty for the light to change, who momentarily pause to recall the author-makers of these found and finding visual narratives as they rehear a story in the head, one the radio told, a long story including details of death and life, thereby causing the passersby, us or any of the others of us who pass us by on these same corners equally regularly, find ourselves listening to and find the calm, possessed, evenly spoken voice so very widely broadcast in our times, as it recounts this tale of inspiration and woe, implying not only the one but the many other invisible others like the one about whom the story is so...if not thoroughly then tellingly told, who make as these author-makers make, leading us to wonder, no...to worry... about how they are doing and if they are living and if they might be well and if it is possible that they are going to be okay, which seems improbable now that we can see, no...hear...that the work they make is experienced like this, like a *reminder*, rather than as than a fact for itself.

Finding these fragments, broken pieces for which we ourselves serve in the role of agents for spreading, can be the cause of a change in course so that instead of fully reaching the spot that is designated as home a walk is taken around the block. There was no *actual* thought that we would find him, but we imagine that we *might*—little is truly impossible, for there is still the park.

The Lover

When you find him, I am shy.
No, when I find him I forget why I needed to find him. No.

When I find him, I am glad for just a moment, then I am shy. I feel
that he is hunchedover.

I don't have a graceful way with him.
I do my best.

He surprises me. I become stiff and uncomfortable in my effort to
master of a moment that has already passed.

What he makes causes me to want to jump.
I hurl his products across the room.

I could use them now. To throw them right back across the room.

All Intentions Are Good

Now comes sadness over the vulnerability of things. Not death, destruction, an action that occurs when its maker energetically moves without resisting easy acquisition. Here he is hypothetical but soon he will become real, attractive when he made it so clear he was looking upon a thing with genuine interest, as it appeared, in the thing itself. For him there are many such things.

He moves with the same assurance as the man he has replaced. Except that he is not that man and he is wheeling a child, something that man did not do. Furthermore the child is in a three-wheeled buggy that is very well-made. The man he has replaced is somewhere, but it is a less apparent place, and now when he walks, he seems less assured.

We might judge it, but for each of us, something analogous to this scenario occurs periodically, in which something has to go, or die, or undergo whatever happens when a thing is replaced.

Afterwards he says he did not mean it, any of it, and that he is sorry for the thing how injured it's become, how injured and uninteresting.

The Lover

To look at a lover from any angle is the meaning of love. I am restating something Picasso said when I say that beauty is monumental when the absurd grotesque of one angle meets in forceful equality the graceful dignity of another. In a lover that is being looked at from any angle these positions are mobile. This is the meaning of love. We are wary, in this case (for, we are wary in general), of parts that fit together too neatly. We cannot bear suffering without a show, a paroxysm. The paroxysm outsizes our container. Our container explodes, we refit accordingly. It can't be easy; I take it we must be born with or learn to develop strong hearts.

Still, we often feel as though we could die of this world; we often do.

Love Everyone

Language and knowledge are not mutually exclusive. I suspect that we knew then what we know now but could not utter it, for then our *markings* would be utterances rather than material objects and like I said, we were clear in our intentions at least among ourselves.

And yet. We could not keep all the particulars of it, our suffering, within the confines of our chest and breath with which it, our suffering, battled for room to breathe. News of it, in terrible specific detail and formidable monstrous scope, intensifies apace diminishing intervals, ever more frequent arrivals, within which each message, has less *time* to settle, to make for itself a place, whilst taking up more *space* due to containing more information than the one which came gunning toward us such a short time before the one that barrels us down so immediately, that is directly, after. Clamorous competing onslaughts knock the wind out of our only just budding not yet blossoming organs of considerate response. No matter. Whether we have the chance or don't to grow our organs into maturity, develop into full bloom, finely tune our considering machines—utilize whichever metaphor repels you least—the fact is we cannot access the time or space sufficient for them to execute their intelligent and biological response.

We worry that our circuits will blow.

We resist.

We need to find our circuits; we need our circuits.

We resist.

We haven't yet connected with our helping hand.

Even now, long after the accident and its consequences, it causes me great grief to consider the complex progression of mutated thinking that seduces us to naively grow the enemy camp—a deranged scene we watch and wince over, over and over, the repeat play of us assisting our invaders, providing them with such smooth travel along paths otherwise foreign to them but well-known to us, providing the luxury of avoiding a wrong turn, such an obvious hazard of movement so banal even they anticipate it as a necessary derailment from an otherwise starkly uninterruptable advance upon the finally abundant tapestry of our no longer spheric world. As we loose ourselves from the potency for thriving that our invaders do therefore acquire from our not quite happy nor hopeful, but foolishly spirited acquiescence, we position our actions as somehow supporting ourselves on our way to a multiple, luminous yet undefined perhaps to be forever unknown path of becoming.

Were we then not unlike the preceding generations, people and governments of long ago 'kneeling like sheep' at the moment of brutal annexations and programmatic annihilations? We drove so far into our delusional fantasy of benefitting from the incursions of our oppressors that we not only complied with their demands as they confronted us, we *anticipated* future requirements, thinking that doing so represented a kind of forward thinking which would allow us *simultaneity* with our opposite, an aggregated, accelerated and ecological evolution forceful enough to fully flip the miserable event befalling us into one made remarkable by an opening in which to *spare* us, and by its structural potential to alleviate for us the circularity of failed attempts and frustrated desires to think or formulate a vision into a thing lasting *beyond* its initiation. We project the power of our foe as a power that put to *our* use will solve our chronic memory loss, relieve us the tragedy of interminable repeat, and illogically if not miraculously allow them, our perpetrators, to find their way toward the advance of some *true and eternal* if as yet unarticulated longing to build a verdant communal life inhabited by dignity and regard for public and private bodies, alongside us. We would walk together, *they* and *us*, assisting each other—*they*—being the cursed deliverers of our current condition of being returned to a vacated hellish void—*they who*—all together and each *individually*, possess such brute singularity we are unable to permit ourselves knowledge of them even inside of dream or memory for it cannot align with what little we know from the archived history of our (short) life in this world—*and we*—the very bodies for which we imagined such *dignity* and regard; and that this *walk together* would have the potential to transform them, us, into livable, animated, coexistent bodies, improbably shared, by way of building an animated agora and all its manifold parts, including wine, art, philosophy, lovemaking and the intimacy that came with, which would no doubt be the basis of tender care for, growing precious beings, objects and structures that frame and inhabit these streets in and upon which we live and learn to love.

Temptations come increasingly close, reaching us by bridge and landfill across seas now literally stuffed whereupon proximity becomes the problem that occludes the clarity we don't have until the advancing invasion exposes its purpose as something other than soft or erotic touch—as when we, who were speaking, but who lacked that imperative, considered nature in our times, to make others more like ourselves, excitedly took for ourselves the missionary's epochal task, translating "God is Love" or "God Bless You" or "Pass the Grace" into what is now regularly seen exiting our mouths as: *"Love Everyone."*

The implication of this phrase is most significant to us who involuntarily though loudly resist its totality just as it is becoming so total we take *great risk* with who and what we are quickly coming to care most about when we argue amongst ourselves about whom, what and how this now common aphoristic and blithe use of language, *love everyone*, serves. For us, love, *especially* love, held a unique position despite the dearth of our experience as the one uninhibited extreme we might legitimately hope would enable us to exceed our limitation. Holding onto this idea, that Love was nuanced and potentially meaningful, made us look angry and marginal, for if we were not so, we argued, what did we have against it, against loving everyone.

OUTSIDE

(or, Help and The Movies)

We could not know how to live in this world.

It was hard for us to sit tight in situations lacking importance even as we, who were left clueless as to how we came into this world all at once and all one way, could neither trust our sensibilities to read correctly what was important and what wasn't nor imagine that any one event, cause, catastrophe, or solution was more important or real than any other—yes, the toxicity, these noxious burns we got while swimming and walking and the proliferations of mutancy from inside and outside our beleaguered bods. We knew we lived in dire times.

We'd resisted but we fail to deny the pull of the screen, its glowing potency, the pause and intensification of thinking in the dark, being stopped by an image, or the dubious notion that an image would be *lent* to us to fill out our incomplete picture-sense of things. We cannot help but be seduced into the conviction that what we view is our own reality—it is *conjured* to be real to us, up closer, close so the face is this big we think it *must be* our face and so green, as seen from the perspective of that face, a child's, it must be what *we* saw as children, although we cannot conceive of ourselves as children, and this is how we walk with a song in our head or feel vulnerable and exposed under the yellow of gaudy urban light, and the uttered becomes the indelible whether it is merely vagary or actual memory:

—*Don't go out tonight. Something's happening out there. Be bloody you know?*
—*When black people were attacked before, and defended themselves, you didn't used to stay in and have your supper.*

Toward a watery room in which the three of them make love, then turn to dust, in a final frame burning itself from center where she is both tiny and impossibly, ever increasingly, large, relaxing upon the monumental neon sign while shifting our understanding of her race, immigration, Vietnam, and he is bathing in a tub, the sole object of a floor, cavernous and raw, in which he is never alone.

She skates around him.

He is in danger.

We are ourselves *encased* in the moldy furniture *popping* stale and over-salted pieces into mouths where we are in a terrific dark at high noon on a balmy summer day watching a wall upon which already someone has died causing us the urge to place our hand on a leg beside us knowing that although we are together in our consuming absorption of what we do and have seen, we, each of us, is in front of him and her, against them, are alone, left there by the absence of a gesture.

"To get at a image without gestures is to get at it as idea." Already however another image and another have projected and passed, faster than the train or truck, delivering goods; simultaneously going back and forth.

Ever theory.

Always bird.

Outside the birds sing. They do not sing the same all day.

Were we not asked to say I, and another? Inside in the theater. On the sand-colored plain.

Where birds are not singing or yes singing but the same at any time of day.

Birds imply, are implied in, what fails, where falls.

Outside limit of the human.

Group is resistance, to enchancement, blooms in the crevice.

We missed what we had not had,
recalled in a place we had not been,
failed to recognize places we should have known well.

Who can fault us our pleasure in déjà vu.

Bodies release form, release to group, realize form out from slight opening into now seen, not open.

We get there. There is a mistake to our approach so we forget why we came. Why did we think this route was a good idea. While we were making the mistake, we heard a massive siren scream. Nothing was reported and it mattered less.

These paths over-determined and criminal have finally been abandoned and we are bicycling around the landing fields now. At an airport that no longer flies. We cannot say 'things'; they happen in the directions of fold, of skin.

Since all of us are the same none of us serve. Disobedience is neutralized in the absence of the mischief required. (This makes us very loud and lonely again.) Air holds us while we move through it down toward our fall into the ruins, the rubble shakes us, we are dutifully transformed, here, at a future, watchers wandering in the surrounds.

Bird continues to sing in between clouds hued soft; they are hardly white.

She is our accident, our open, bird bird-like, brittle, only gestural so she cannot stand. That is literal. She cannot stand.

No Accidents... Acknowledgements

Sections of the novel in previous form were generously and gorgeously published by these editors in these publications: Micaela Morrissette/*Web Conjunctions*, Cara Benson/*Sous Rature*, E. Tracy Grinnell/*Aufgabe*, Laura Elrick/*The Portable Boog Reader*, Kate Zambreno/*Everyday Genius,* Evan Lavender-Smith/*Puerto Del Sol*, Ana Božičević & Amy King/*Revolution-Esque*, Krystal Languell/*Bone Bouquet*, Laynie Brown, Teresa Carmody/*I'll Drown My Book*.

I am deeply indebted to Renee Gladman, Gail Scott and Christian Hawkey, and to my luminous editors Dan Machlin and Jennifer Tamayo, all of whom performed numerous, defining, loving readings.

This book is framed by many engagements, its making enabled by a multitude of writers and lovers and friends, especially conversations about and readings of experimental prose (baroque, new narrative, excessive, conceptual, etc.) and conversations that anticipate a coming radical activism and politics, many of which were had with Nicolas Veroli,

Akilah Oliver (1961-2011), Dana Greene, Tisa Bryant and the brave inventors of the Belladonna* Collaborative.

Thank you to Andrea Trimarco who, in 2005 instructed me to "write a novel" about the accident just when I encountered its accompanying image: it was a blown-up photograph, in a NYC gallery, of young WTO protesters, up close and unwritten, inviting.

This book is dedicated to those protesters, the spaces they made then and since, to Alma Marlena Wolf, to the future, and its mothers.

$16.00

ISBN 978-0-9822798-2-3

51600>

9 780982 279823